Jake the Snake

and the

Stupid Time-Out Chair

Shelly Faith Nicholson

Illustrated by: Colleen Konieczny

PublishAmerica
Baltimore

First printing

ISBN: 1-60836-687-1 (softcover)
ISBN: 978-1-4489-6944-9 (hardcover)
PUBLISHED BY PUBLISHAMERICA, LLLP
www.publishamerica.com
Baltimore

Printed in the United States of America

TO:
The real Jake the Snake,
his big brothers Johnny and Evan,
and his little sister Halie

In memory of Michael Comfort,
Illustrator Colleen Konieczny's inspirational art teacher

Acknowledgments

Thank you John, for supporting my dreams of creating this book. Thank you Johnny, Evan, Jacob and Halie for listening and laughing while I proofread my story. To Jacob William Nicholson, whose everyday antics inspired me to write this book. Without you, there would be no Jake The Snake! To Jake's big brother Johnny and the pet lizard that didn't really drowned in chocolate sauce, but really did die. Rest in peace, Geico. To Evan and Halie. I love you! To my little neighbor, Kelsey, who was inspiration for the character Chelsea Mayer. A huge thanks goes to my illustrator, Colleen Konieczny, who spent many, many hours working to bring Jake The Snake to life with her beautiful illustrations! To Colleen's six beautiful children. A huge thanks goes to my sister Susie, who loaned me her computer when mine was broken and has always been supportive of my writing efforts. To the owner of Furnace Hill Photography, Joni Morrison, who also happens to be my sister-in-law, for the back cover photograph. To Santa Claus, who I'll always believe in. And to all the kids who will read my book. I hope Jake the Snake will make you laugh!

Table of Contents

1. The Stupid Time-Out Chair

My name is Jake. Except I like to be called Jake the Snake. Everyone calls me that name. 'Cause Mom and Dad say it's a catchy nickname. Except sometimes my big brother Johnny just calls me *Stupid Kid*. I don't even like that dumb name though.

I like snakes. Plus other slimy things like toads and lizards. Johnny has a pet lizard. His name is Larry.

My age is five and three-quarters. I go to the half-day kind of school. It's real name is Kindergarten. That's where people learn their '*P's*' and '*Q's*'. Plus learn how to add up numbers. And sometimes do show and tell. Johnny goes to the all day kind of school. He has to do lots of stupid homework. Plus he says his teacher is real bad mean. I'm more lucky. 'Cause I have a real nice teacher. Her name is Mrs. Hurley. She's kind of old like Grandma. But she's real fun for being an old woman. She's lots chubbier than Grandma too. But Mom says I shouldn't ever say she's old and chubby. 'Cause that ain't very nice.

I have a girlfriend at that Kindergarten too. Her name is Chelsea Mayer. She sits at my table. She has pretty curly hair. Plus she wears two bows in her hair. Sometimes those bows are pink. And sometimes those bows have plastic puppy dog heads in the middle. The puppy dog ones are my favoritest. Chelsea Mayer is real cute. That's why I try to hug her. Sometimes I even try to kiss Chelsea Mayer. Except she doesn't even like it when I try the kissing part.

"No, Jake the Snake! Leave me alone! I don't want any kisses!"

"But you're my girlfriend, Chelsea Mayer! So you have to kiss me!"

"I am not your girlfriend, Jake the Snake! Leave me alone, you stinky boy!"

Except I don't even know why she calls me *Stinky Boy*. 'Cause I don't even smell bad. Mom makes me take a bath every night, whether I like it or not.

Then the bad part happens. Chelsea Mayer tells Mrs. Hurley, "Jake the Snake is trying to kiss me! Make him stop!"

That's called tattle telling. Mom says tattle telling ain't very nice.

Except Mrs. Hurley must not know that rule. 'Cause she doesn't even tell Chelsea Mayer it's not nice. Instead she tells me, "There is no kissing allowed in school!"

Except I think that's a real dumb rule.

Then the separating part happens. That's when Mrs. Hurley puts me at a table where Chelsea Mayer ain't sitting. That's kind of like being put in time-out.

Mom puts me in time-out lots at home. Except not for kissing her. She puts me in time-out when I'm a bad kid. There's a chair in the corner of the living room. That's where I go when I'm bad. Except I don't like sitting in that stupid time-out chair. It's real boring. Plus I don't like sitting there for a more worse reason. It's almost Christmas. I know that 'cause there's a bunch of snow on the ground. So guess what that means? It means Santa's coming soon, that's what! I know Santa sees me sitting in that stupid time-out chair. 'Cause everyone knows that guy sees you if you're good or bad. He has some kind of magic eyes, I think.

Except if you're a bad kid, he doesn't even bring gifts on Christmas. He brings a big lump of coal instead.

Except that's a stupid gift. 'Cause what can you do with a big black rock? If I had a rock collection, it might be nice. Except that's a problem. Cause I ain't a rock collector. Plus Johnny won't even share his new toys. 'Cause he doesn't even like to share. So I'll just be stuck with a stupid black rock.

2. The Big Shiny Light

Saturday is my favoritest day of the week. Saturday is almost as good as Christmas. 'Cause I don't even have to go to stupid Kindergarten on Saturday. And Johnny doesn't have to go to the all day kind of school. Except he never wants to play with me. He just draws pictures by himself. Sometimes I ask him to share his markers.

But he always says, "No, Stupid Kid! You'll leave the caps off! And they'll dry out!"

Sometimes Johnny just plays video games all day. Except Mom and Dad say that makes people have dead brain cells.

My favoritest thing to do on Saturday is watch Animal World on TV. There are lots of monkeys on that funny show. I like monkeys as much as I like slimy things. 'Cause one time Mom and Dad took me and Johnny to the zoo. And a big baboon monkey stuck its butt on its cage. Then it turned around and spit at us.

"Hey Johnny! Animal World is on! Come watch Animal World with me! There's a monkey on! A big baboon monkey!"

Except Johnny didn't even answer. So I yelled in my loudest yelling voice ever, "Johnny! COME WATCH ANIMAL WORLD WITH ME!"

Except guess what? Johnny still didn't answer. So I ran to Johnny's room. I banged on his bedroom door real hard.

"Johnny! There are monkeys on Animal World! Let's play monkeys. You pretend you're one of those funny baboon monkeys. And I'll pretend I'm one of those little monkeys that swing in the trees." I yelled.

Johnny finally opened his door. First he gave me a real ugly look. Then he started laughing, "Okay, Stupid Kid, I'll play along. Go swing off the chandelier in the dining room. That's what stupid monkeys do. I dare you!"

Johnny slammed his bedroom door in my face.

So that's when I went to the dining room. I looked up at the ceiling. That big shiny light looked like lots of fun to swing on. I climbed up on the big wood table. I jumped up real high. My hands grabbed that shiny chandelier. Then I swung.

"Weeeee! This is fun!" I hollered. "Johnny! Come look at me!"

I swung back and forth a bunch of times. "Woo Who!" I cheered. Except then the bad part happened.

CRASH! SLAM! THUD! SHATTER! That whole big shiny chandelier came off the ceiling. It hit the table with a monster BANG! All those light bulbs broke in a billion zillion pieces.

Johnny came running out of his room. Mom came running out of the laundry room. Dad came running out of the garage. Everybody looked at me real ugly. I gave Mom and Dad the puppy dog look. That's when I pucker my bottom lip way far out.

"Jake the Snake!" Mom screamed.

"Jake the Snake!" Dad hollered.

"HA HA HA!" laughed Johnny.

"You could have been seriously injured!" Dad said.

"You need to sit in the time-out chair and think about what you did!" Mom said.

"Stupid Kid!" Johnny said.

Mom and Dad sent Johnny to his room.

My eyes leaked a bunch of tears. 'Cause I was real scared. Then I promised Mom and Dad I wouldn't ever do that again. 'Cause I could have been real bad hurt. Maybe even deader than a doornail. Plus I promised I'd be a good kid till Christmas. 'Cause I just knew Santa saw it all.

3. The Messy Sandcastle

One day after school I was real wound up. 'Cause Mom showed me the calendar.

"Look, Jake the Snake! Only 14 days until Santa comes!"

I jumped up and down. I zoomed all over the place.

"If you calm down," Mom said, "we'll bake some cookies for Santa."

I thought that was the bestest idea ever. 'Cause I knew Santa loved cookies. That guy's got a real fat belly, that's why.

I helped Mom use the rolling pin. Except I spilled some white floury stuff on my shirt.

"Go change your shirt while the cookies are baking," Mom said, "and please remember to put your dirty shirt in the hamper."

Except when I went to the laundry room, the hamper was all filled up. So I thought I'd be a real big help to Mom. Plus maybe even get my name on Santa's good kid list. I watched Mom wash clothes a billion zillion times before. It looked real easy. Santa would put me on his good kid list for sure if I did Mom's laundry. So I dumped the hamper on the floor. I stuffed all the clothes in the washer machine. Then I jammed them down real good with the end of Mom's broom handle. They all fit.

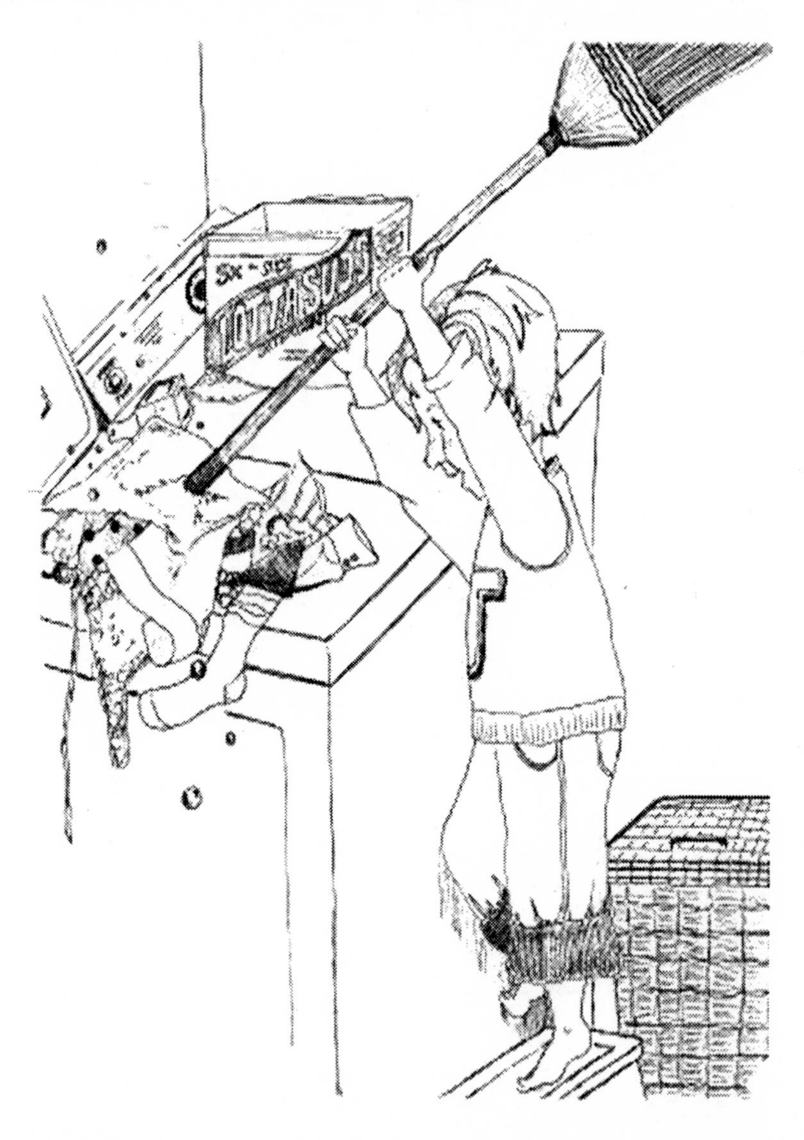

I took three giant scoops of that powdery laundry cleaning stuff. Then my brain got a real smart idea. That broom handle looked like a giant stirring stick. So I stirred all that powdery stuff in with the dirty clothes. Except I spilled a bunch on the floor. That stuff looked pretty neat. It looked like sand at the beach. Except it came with its own scooper and everything. I wondered if Mom ever built sandcastles when she did laundry.

Then my brain got another real good idea. I stood on the step stool. I filled the scooper thing with water from the sink. I poured some of the water in that box with the powdery laundry cleaning stuff. Then I found my sand bucket. I filled it with a bunch of powdery stuff. I packed it down real good. Then I dumped it on the floor. It looked just like a sandcastle! Except it needed some decorations. So I stuck my hand down in the washer machine. I felt around real good. I pulled out one of Dad's dirty handkerchiefs. Except first I made sure there wasn't no snot on it. I stuck it right on top of that sandcastle. It made a super good flag.

That's when Mom started hollering, "The cookies are done!"

I ran to the kitchen real fast. I made a special announcement to Mom. "I have a surprise for you in the laundry room! Come see!"

Except Mom got a real funny look on her face. Then she followed me real fast.

"Surprise!" I yelled. "I did all the laundry! Plus I made a sandcastle for you!"

Mom's face turned a funny color. She made her eyes real squinty. Plus she pointed her pointer finger at me. "YOUNG MAN! TO THE TIME-OUT CHAIR THIS INSTANT!" she hollered.

I guess Mom didn't even like her nice surprise. 'Cause she called me *Young Man.* That's the name she calls me when she's real mad.

I sat and sat a real long time in that stupid time-out chair. I heard Mom making a bunch of loud noises. It sounded like she was fighting with a giant monster. Except I know there ain't no such thing. Then the noise got quiet. But just for a second. 'Cause then I heard a big booming sound. *BOOM! BOOM! BOOM!*

Maybe it *was* a monster! I hid my eyes behind my hands. I peeked through my fingers real nervous. *BOOM! BOOM! BOOM!* Maybe the monster ate Mom. Maybe I was its dessert. I felt real scared. I squeezed my eyes shut real tight. Except then I peeked. 'Cause I couldn't even help it. The booming noise was Mom's mad feet. Her feet went *STOMP BOOM STOMP* on the hard floor. I was real happy it wasn't a monster. Except Mom had a scary monster look on her face. Mom stomped over to the stupid time-out chair. She shook her pointer finger at me. Then she gave me a real good lecture. That's what grown-ups call yelling at kids.

"YOU MADE A BIG MESS, YOUNG MAN!" Mom yelled. "YOU WILL SIT IN THE TIME-OUT CHAIR UNTIL DAD GETS HOME FROM WORK!"

I felt real mad at Mom.

That's when my brain told me to say something real mean.

"I wish I had a new Mom!" I said. "'Cause you're the meanest mom in the whole world!"

Mom looked at me kind of sad.

That'll teach you, Lady! I thought in my brain.

Except then Mom said something that made me real scared. "Maybe you can ask Santa for a new Mom. I bet he has lots of moms at the North Pole."

Except I didn't really want a new Mom. So I started to cry. I cried myself to sleep, right there in that stupid time-out chair.

Except then a yummy smell woke up my nostrils. I opened my eyes. Dad was home. Mom was cooking dinner. It was my favorite. Spaghetti and meatballs. Mom was the best. I *really* didn't want a new North Pole Mom. What if Santa heard me? What if he brought me a new North Pole Mom instead of a lump of coal?

I ran to the kitchen real fast. I hugged Mom real tight.

"What was that for?" Mom asked.

"It's 'cause I don't even want a new North Pole Mom. I'm sorry I made a mess."

"Santa's not going to bring you a new North Pole Mom," Mom said. "I will always be your Mom. Whether you like it or not."

Mom kissed my forehead. "I'm sorry I lost my temper." she said.

I felt real bad Mom lost her temper.

"Where'd you lose it, Mom? I can help you find it."

Mom giggled. "No, Jake the Snake. It just means I was angry with you."

Then Mom got the bestest idea ever. "After dinner I'll help you write a letter to Santa. Maybe you can ask for a sand table. Then you can build non-messy sandcastles!"

Except after Mom helped me write that letter, I did something else real bad. So Santa might erase me off that good kid list again. Plus I'll probably still get a stupid lump of coal.

4. The Shaving Cream Snowman

Johnny made a real neat picture of a puffy snowman at his school.

"How did you make it, Johnny?" I asked.

"We mixed shaving cream with glue and painted the snowman," Johnny said. "Then we cut out scraps of felt for the scarf. My teacher gave us some buttons to glue on the snowman's jacket."

"I want to make one too!" I said.

Johnny rolled his eyes. "Then make one, Stupid Kid! Just don't touch mine!"

"Name calling isn't nice!" Mom said in a real grouchy voice. "Why don't you share some of your paper and markers with Jake the Snake? Then he can draw a snowman too."

"Fine," Johnny said.

Except I didn't even want to *draw* a snowman. I wanted to make a shaving cream one. Just like Johnny's.

I took the paper Johnny gave me upstairs to my bedroom. I laid it on my art table. Then I went in the bathroom. I saw Dad's shaving cream way up high on the shelf. Except I couldn't even reach it. Then I saw a bottle of Mom's smelly lotion sitting by the sink.

My brain thought lotion would work just as good. Plus my snowman would even smell good. Just like Mom.

So I took Mom's lotion to my bedroom. I got the bottle of glue out of my craft box. I mixed up the lotion with the glue. Then I painted a snowman on the paper.

Except I still needed some cloth for the scarf. Plus I needed some buttons for its belly. I wanted my picture to look just like Johnny's.

My brain got the bestest idea ever. 'Cause I saw my fancy suit jacket hanging up in my closet. That was the fanciest jacket ever. 'Cause it had real shiny buttons. They looked like rich people's gold or something.

So I took the purple safety scissors out of my craft box. Safety scissors are the kind that don't make you bleed if you jab yourself. I climbed up on my step stool. Then I cut those buttons off.

Then I found my dress-up tie. I wear that thing to church. Except I don't really like it. 'Cause it makes my neck scratchy. I thought it would make a real perfect scarf for my snowman. Except it was way too long. So I tried to cut a little piece out of it. Except those stupid safety scissors weren't even sharp enough. So I just glued the whole tie onto my snowman's neck.

My snowman was lots snazzier than Johnny's!

I heard Mom humming a Christmas tune. She walked in my bedroom. She had a big stack of clean laundry in a basket.

"Look, Mom! I made a snowman picture just like Johnny's!" I held my picture way high up so she could see it.

Except I don't think Mom liked it. She threw those clothes way high up in the air. Her face got all white. She looked like she saw a scary ghost. Except I know there ain't no such thing. She grabbed the bottle of smelly lotion. Plus she grabbed my scratchy dress-up tie.

Mom's face turned real purplish. Then she yelled in her loudest yelling voice ever, "THIS IS MY BOTTLE OF EXPENSIVE LOTION! AND JUST LOOK AT YOUR GOOD TIE, YOUNG MAN!"

She called me *Young Man* again. That ain't ever a good sign.

"I'm sorry, Mom," I said. I did the puppy dog look.

She picked up my snowman picture. Then she pulled one of those fancy buttons off my snowman's belly. A big blue bump popped out up above her nose. Her face turned real bright red.

She pointed her pointer finger to the staircase. And guess what that meant? To the stupid time-out chair for me, that's what.

UH OH! Santa was going to be real mad this time! I bet he'd cancel the sand table request.

5. Show and Tell

Mrs. Hurley made a big announcement at my Kindergarten. "Tomorrow is the last day of school before Christmas vacation. We will be having a special show and tell!"

Everybody got real quiet. 'Cause everybody wanted to hear what kind of special show and tell Mrs. Hurley was talking about.

"We will be talking about pets tomorrow. Please bring a photo of your pet."

I waved my hand in the air.

"Yes, Jake the Snake?" Mrs. Hurley asked.

"My brother Johnny has a pet lizard. His name is Larry. Can I bring Larry to school?"

"That would be lovely," Mrs. Hurley said.

Chelsea Mayer smiled at me. "I never saw a real live lizard before. That's neat."

I grinned back at Chelsea Mayer. I bet Chelsea Mayer would want to be my girlfriend after she saw Larry.

The next day I was real happy. 'Cause guess why? Johnny told me I could take Larry the Lizard to school.

Except Mom had to give Johnny an ugly look first. Plus she had to tell him it was real mean not to share.

I was real happy for another reason too. Mom said we were going to make chocolate covered pretzels after I got home from Kindergarten. Chocolate pretzels! Plus show and tell! And Chelsea Mayer was going to be my girlfriend! It was the bestest day of my whole entire life!

Then Johnny said in a mean voice, "*DO NOT* take Larry out of his cage!"

"Why not?" I asked.

"Because, Stupid Kid, if he gets loose he might crawl up your teacher's leg. And then he'll crawl in her underwear. Or he might crawl onto one of your little baby friends. And that'll make them cry!"

"My friends aren't babies, Johnny!"

"Except then Mom yelled, "Name calling isn't nice! Get ready for school instead of calling each other names!"

"I don't want the stupid kid to lose Larry," Johnny said.

"I'm sure Jake the Snake will take good care of Larry," Mom patted the top of my head. "Won't you, Jake the Snake?"

I smiled and nodded. Then I stuck my tongue out at Johnny. Except I did that part when Mom wasn't even looking.

I had to wait a real long time for my turn at show and tell. My bestest friend named Patrick brought a picture of his big yellow dog, Buttercup. Samantha, the red-haired girl, brought her black guinea pig. It looked like a big rat without the creepy tail. Except it didn't even eat cheese. It ate lettuce. Alex brought a picture of his pet pony. I thought that was the neatest pet ever. One time I asked Mom and Dad for a pony. Except Dad said we didn't have room for it. I thought it could live in the garage with my bike. Except Dad said, "No!" 'Cause he didn't want it to stink up the place. So I got a rocking pony instead. It wasn't as neat as a real live pony though.

My turn was next after Chelsea Mayer's. Chelsea Mayer didn't even have a pet. So she brought a baby doll instead. It was the kind that burped when you whacked it on the back. Except I don't even like stupid baby dolls. They're for girls only.

When Mrs. Hurley finally called my name I went up front. I was kind of scared. 'Cause there were lots of kids in that room, that's why.

"What did you bring to show us, Jake the Snake?"

"I brought Johnny's lizard," I said. "His name is Larry."

"Can you tell us something about Larry?" Mrs. Hurley asked.

"Sometimes he's green and sometimes he's brown," I said. "He turns brown when he's scared of stuff. Or if you pick him up by his tail. Or shake his cage."

Everybody looked real interested. I didn't feel so scared anymore.

"He's green when he's happy," I said. "Like when he's out of this stupid cage. Except don't even ask me to take him out. 'Cause Johnny will be mad if he gets loose. Plus

Mrs. Hurley will be mad if Larry crawls up her underwear."

Everybody laughed at that. Except Mrs. Hurley. Her face turned real pink.

I wondered if Santa would be mad I said that.

After show and tell, Mrs. Hurley passed out coloring books. They had pictures of Santa jumping down a chimney on the front. My brain thought Mrs. Hurley was real nice to give us those books.

After that, Chelsea Mayer gave me a candy cane. She asked me if I wanted to hold her stupid baby doll so she could look at Larry.

"Baby dolls are stupid." I said. "They're for girls only."

"Boys are stupid too," said Chelsea Mayer. "And stinky."

I guessed she didn't want to be my girlfriend after all. I felt kind of sad about that.

Except then I cheered up. 'Cause Mom came to pick me up. I remembered we were going home to make yummy chocolate pretzels. Plus there wouldn't be any more school till after Christmas!

Except when we got home something real bad happened. So maybe that would mean no Christmas gifts for me anyhow. Maybe it would mean a stupid black rock instead.

6. Larry and the Chocolate Sauce

When we got home, Mom told me to put Larry's cage away. 'Cause she was going to melt chocolate for the pretzels.

I hung up my coat. Then I ran to Johnny's bedroom real fast with the lizard cage. Except that's when the bad part happened. I looked in the cage. Larry wasn't there!

If Larry was lost, Johnny was going to kill me. I decided I'd better look for Larry. So I opened the top of that cage real careful. I stuck my hand down in the wood chips. Lizards like wood chips. 'Cause that's where they poop. I felt around real good. Except I tried not to grab no lizard poop. Then Larry surprised me. He jumped right out of those wood chips. He landed on my shirt. Except that was bad news. 'Cause I never even held Larry all by myself before. I was scared he had real sharp teeth. I was scared he'd bite my finger off. Then blood would squirt all over the place.

"HELP, MOM! HELP! LARRY IS STUCK TO MY SHIRT!" I yelled.

Except Mom didn't even answer.

I ran real fast to the kitchen. Mom wasn't there. Larry was still hanging on. Then the bad part happened. He must've smelled that yummy chocolate sauce melting on the stove. 'Cause he took one giant hop off my shirt. And he dived right into that pot of ooey gooey chocolate sauce. I saw him swim around a little bit. Except then he disappeared. It was just like magic. Except I knew it wasn't. I was real scared.

Mom walked in the kitchen. "Were you calling me?" she asked.

My brain had to think of something real quick. So I told a fib. But just a little white fib. That's what a not real bad fib is called.

"Who me? No, I wasn't calling you," I said.

"I must have been hearing things." Mom giggled. "Are you ready to make pretzels?" she asked.

Mom looked in the pot. She stirred the chocolate around.

My stomach felt kind of pukey.

"I think it's all melted," she said.

Except she didn't even see Larry. 'Cause he already disappeared.

I think my face looked sick. 'Cause Mom asked if I felt okay. Then she felt my head.

"You don't feel warm. But you look awfully pale," Mom said. "Do you have to throw up?"

"I don't know," I said.

"Maybe you'd better lie down," Mom said, "You can taste a few pretzels after you feel better."

Except I didn't even want to taste no pretzels with lizard guts in them. I went to my room. I flopped down on my bed. I covered my head with my pillow. Then the bad part happened. I heard a real loud scream.

"*EEEEEEEEEEK!*"

UH OH! I hoped Mom was just screaming cause she saw a mouse or something. Mom is real scared of mice. 'Cause one time she saw one in the kitchen. She jumped up on the chair. Then she screamed in her loudest screaming voice ever. Dad had to step on that thing. He squashed it deader than a doornail. Except it was real gross. 'Cause he had mouse guts stuck to the bottom of his shoe.

Except guess what? It wasn't a mouse. 'Cause I heard Mom yell in her loudest yelling voice ever, "JACOB SYLVESTER NELSON! GET DOWNSTAIRS THIS MINUTE!"

Jacob Sylvester Nelson is my whole real name. Except I don't even like my middle name of Sylvester. 'Cause Sylvester is an old people's name. That's 'cause I was named after my Great Grandpa Sylvester. And he's real old. Mom only calls me my whole real name when she's real super mad. Being called *Jacob Sylvester Nelson* is even more worse than being called *Young Man.*

I was real scared. So I put on the worstest puppy dog face ever. I walked real slow down those stairs.

I hid my face behind my hands. I walked into the kitchen real slow. I peeked through my fingers. Mom was holding a big spoon with holes in it. Larry was laying on the spoon with his legs up in the air. There was chocolate sauce dripping off him. He looked deader than a doornail. I think he ate too much chocolate.

"HOW DID LARRY GET IN THE CHOCOLATE SAUCE?" Mom screeched.

That's when tears started leaking out of my eyes. I told Mom the whole story. She looked at me. Then she laid dead Larry on a napkin. Except the next part surprised me. 'Cause Mom hugged me.

"Why didn't you tell me Larry fell in the chocolate sauce?" Mom asked.

"'Cause I was scared you'd put me in that stupid time-out chair. Except now I'm just scared Johnny's going to kill me!" A big hurting hiccup came out of my mouth. 'Cause that's what happens when I cry lots.

"Johnny's not going to kill you," Mom said. Then she patted my back. "Everything will be okay. I promise."

"Can I go sit in the stupid time-out chair now?" I cried.

"You don't have to," Mom said. "You're not in trouble."

"I know. I just want to," I said.

Mom looked at me kind of sad.

"Okay, Sweetie," she said.

So I put myself in time-out. I wondered if Santa would still count it.

Mom had to throw away all those yummy chocolate pretzels. I was sad 'cause Larry was deader than a doornail. Except I was more sad all the chocolate pretzels had lizard guts in them.

When Johnny got home from the all day kind of school, Mom broke the dead lizard news to him. Tears leaked out of Johnny's eyes. Mom told Johnny that Larry was in lizard heaven. Except I didn't even know that place existed.

"Please don't be mad at Jake the Snake," Mom told Johnny. "It was just an accident. He loved Larry as much as you did."

Johnny gave me a real ugly look. Except I didn't even care. 'Cause I felt real sorry for him.

Then Mom got the bestest idea ever, "When Dad comes home from work, let's go chop down a Christmas Tree!"

Johnny's eyes quit leaking tears. Christmas Trees make everything better.

7. The Shiny Star

We always wait till the last minute to cut down a Christmas Tree. That's 'cause Mom and Dad say all those needles fall off. Plus they get stuck in the carpet. Then they jag at our feet. 'Cause they're as sharp as tacks, that's why. Plus Mom says they clog up the vacuum cleaner. Then Dad has to take it apart with a screwdriver. Then he says bad words.

We looked at all the trees at that Christmas Tree place. The one I liked had a big bare spot. Johnny picked one with brown needles all over the place. Mom liked one that was too tall for our roof.

Then Dad saw one he liked. It had real long needles on it.

Dad said, "This is the perfect tree!"

Except I thought the one I picked was lots better.

Dad looked at the trunk to make sure it wasn't crooked.

'Cause Dad said, "Trees with crooked trunks are no good."

Dad got out his big saw. Mom was scared he'd chop our legs off or something. 'Cause we all stood way far back. Dad tied that giant tree up on top of Mom's car. It was real monster big. I thought Mom's whole car would tip over. Except it didn't. Dad drove real slow so that tree wouldn't fly away.

It took Mom and Dad a real long time to get that tree ready before we could decorate it. Dad pounded it in the tree stand with his hammer. Then he made sure it wasn't crooked. Then Mom and Dad moved the stupid time-out chair to the other corner. They put that giant Christmas Tree in the stupid time-out chair's spot. After Mom put the blinky lights on, me and Johnny hung the shiny balls all over it.

Then I remembered my favorite part. The shiny star!

"Dad! Get the ladder! So we can put the shiny star on top!" I hollered.

"Not tonight, Jake the Snake," Dad said. "We'll do that tomorrow."

"But Dad..." I begged.

"No whining, Jake the Snake. I'm too tired."

Dad gets tired a lot. That's cause he's kind of old. Old people get tired real easy.

Johnny went to his bedroom to do his homework. Mom went to wash more dirty clothes. Dad went to watch TV. Mom calls that being a couch potato.

That star was so shiny. I picked it up. I flipped it over in my hand. Then my brain got the bestest idea ever! I was a real good tree climber. Dad didn't even need that silly ladder. I could put that shiny star on top all by myself! I'd surprise my whole family. Dad wouldn't have to climb that big ladder with his old legs. Mom would be real surprised. That shiny star might even brighten Johnny's day. He'd forget all about dead Larry. So I took that Christmas star in one hand. Then I grabbed onto one of the Christmas tree branches with my other hand. Those long pine needles were real jaggy. Except I didn't even care. 'Cause I couldn't wait to surprise my whole family. Santa would be real happy with me! I climbed and climbed. It seemed real easy. Except when I got to the top, the bad part happened.

That tree started to wobble. It started to shake. The branches started to wiggle. Then that giant tree started to tilt. Some of those shiny balls fell off. Some broke in a billion zillion pieces.

I jumped off real quick. Except when I jumped... *TIMMMBBBER!!!* That whole giant tree fell on the floor with a monster CRASH!

Everybody came running real fast to the living room. My mouth dropped open real wide. 'Cause I couldn't even believe my own eyes.

Mom and Dad had real ugly looks on their faces.

Johnny laughed, "HA! HA! Stupid Kid! You're in big trouble now!"

Mom and Dad sent Johnny to his room. Except I decided that ain't a good time-out place. 'Cause he plays video games in there.

Then Dad pointed his pointer finger to the stupid time-out chair. That's where I stayed. 'Cause Mom and Dad had to fix that broken tree.

"Santa has lots of coal at the North Pole," Mom said.

"Jake the Snake will be lucky if Santa even comes!" Dad said.

That's when my brain decided to be good for the rest of my entire life. 'Cause I didn't even want Santa to bring me no stupid lump of coal. Or even more worse, nothing at all.

I put my pajamas on after Mom and Dad finished the yelling part.

Mom came upstairs to tuck me in bed. That's when my brain got a real good idea.

"Hey, Mom?" I said.

"What is it, Jake the Snake?"

"Will you *please* take me and Johnny to the mall tomorrow?" I begged. "I want to sit on Santa's lap."

"You're afraid to sit on Santa's lap," Mom said.

"I won't be scared tomorrow," I promised. "I have something real important to tell Santa."

"We'll see," Mom said.

Except when Mom says, "*we'll see,*" it really means *No.*

So I did a real good puppy dog face, "*Pleeease*, Mom! I *have* to see Santa! It's real important!"

Mom looked like she was thinking real hard.

"Pretty please?" I put on my worstest puppy dog face ever.

"Okay," Mom answered. "But you'd better be on your best behavior, Young Man!"

"I will. I promise."

Mom kissed the top of my head. “Now go to sleep,” she said.

Except I couldn’t sleep. ’Cause I was real nervous about seeing that big scary guy the next day.

8. The Big Scary Guy

The next morning Mom made dippy eggs for breakfast. Those kind have that runny yellow stuff in the middle. That stuff kind of looks like ear wax. Except it's real yummy. Ear wax tastes real gross. Sometimes I dip my fingers in that runny yellow egg stuff. Except Mom said I should just dip my toast in it. Mom says it makes my muscles real big and strong.

I was in a real big hurry to see that big scary guy. So I ate real fast. Then I ran to my bedroom. I put on my favorite clothes. My blue jeans with my cowboy belt. Plus my yellow shirt with the picture of the horse head on it. I even put on clean action hero underwear. My brain told me to do that. 'Cause Santa sees everything. Then I ran downstairs. I put on my clunky cowboy boots. I bet Santa would love my outfit. 'Cause if Santa likes reindeers I bet he likes horses too. Horses are kind of like reindeers. Except without the horns. Plus they can't fly either.

It took us forever to get to the mall. There were a bunch of red lights. Plus too many cars. Mom said everybody was doing their last minute Christmas shopping. Except I thought those people were real dumb. Everyone knows Christmas happens at the same time every year.

Mom held my hand real tight in the mall. It hurt. Except Mom said it had to hurt so I wouldn't get lost. She pulled me through all the people. We went to the middle of the mall next to the giant Christmas Tree. It had a bunch of giant shiny ball things hanging all over the place. It was as tall as a house. There was a choo choo train running around in a circle. Right in the middle of that choo choo train track was a giant sized chair. It looked like the kind a king would sit in. Except instead of a king sitting there, it was Santa! Plus there were three elves. Except they were tall elves. Not short elves like the ones at the North Pole. And their ears weren't even pointy. Except they did have shoes with curly toes. And jingle bells on their hats.

The line to see Santa was ten miles long. I couldn't even wait. I kept jumping up and down so I could get a real good look at that big scary guy.

Except Mom said, "Stop fidgeting, Jake the Snake!"

Johnny had a real good idea. "Can't we go for ice cream then come back?" he asked.

"The line will just get longer if we don't wait," Mom said.

"How much longer?" I asked kind of whiny.

Mom let out a real big breath. "Be patient!" she said.

"Being patient is boring!" Except I shouldn't have even said that out loud. 'Cause Mom gave me a real mean look.

Johnny rolled his eyes. Except I didn't even care. 'Cause I knew what I was going to tell Santa. I bet after I talked to the big scary guy, he would fly his reindeers to my house. Plus not even bring a stupid lump of coal.

It was finally my turn. My stomach felt kind of funny. It felt like there was a little guy in there doing somersaults. Santa looked real big and scary. I didn't really like his white bushy beard. I wondered why he didn't shave it off. A bunch of other little kids didn't like it either. 'Cause lots of them screamed when they sat on his lap. I decided I'd leave him some of Dad's shaving cream on Christmas Eve. Then he could shave. 'Cause lots of other kids would leave him milk and cookies. And he was fat enough already.

I tried not to be scared. I worked up lots of brave stuff inside my body. My legs felt kind of shaky. I climbed up on that big scary guy's lap. I felt like tears were going to leak out of my eyes. Except I blinked them back.

"Hello, little boy. Have you been good this year?" Santa asked.

OH NO! That was the question I was scared he was going to ask.

I wondered if I should fib. Except my brain told me not to. Cause Santa would put me on the bad kid list for sure. Especially if I fibbed right to his face.

So I told the truth. "Not really," I said kind of shaky. "'Cause I made my brother's lizard drowned in chocolate sauce."

"Will you bring Johnny a new lizard?" I asked. "I'm sorry Larry is deader than a doornail."

Santa looked at me. He laughed real loud. His belly really did shake like jelly.

Santa laughed for a real long time. I didn't even think he'd ever stop. Except he finally did.

"I'll see what I can do for Johnny," Santa said. "Is there anything you'd like for yourself?"

My brain couldn't think. 'Cause I was so scared. So I just said, "Don't bring me no stupid lump of coal. And don't bring me no new North Pole Mom. 'Cause I like the one I got!"

Then I let Santa know how sorry I was for all the bad stuff.

"I promise I'll be a good boy for the rest of my entire life. 'Cause I didn't mean to do any of that bad stuff. Like knock down the Christmas Tree. Or mix Mom's smelly lotion with glue. Or cut those fancy buttons off my jacket. Plus it was real bad to make a sandcastle with that powdery laundry cleaning stuff. And swing off that chandelier thing like a monkey. And I promise I'll never try to kiss Chelsea Mayer again. Or say Mrs. Hurley is old and chubby. And I'm sorry I made Mrs. Hurley's face turn pink. 'Cause I said Larry the Lizard would crawl in her underwear."

Santa looked at me real strange. Then he started to shake. His belly shook a bunch. He even snorted like a pig. His face turned real bright red. Plus his eyes leaked a bunch of tears. Then his mouth sprayed some spit. He shook harder and harder. It looked like his belly was going to explode. I was scared Santa guts were going to fly everywhere. I didn't even want no Santa guts to splatter me in the face! Then Santa would be deader than a doornail. Just like Larry. That would mean no gifts for anyone. Plus no lump of coal.

That's when the bad part happened. My stomach felt real sick. My brain knew barf was going to fly. So I covered my mouth up with my hands.

That's when one of those tall mall elves saw me. She saved the day. 'Cause she took the jingle bell hat off her head. Then she put it under my mouth. I barfed in that tall mall elf's hat.

Santa quit shaking. I was glad. 'Cause he didn't even explode. Except his face turned white. He looked like he was going to barf too. I was real scared. Tears started leaking out of my eyes. The tall mall elf picked me up. She carried me back to Mom. Mom picked me up and hugged me. I felt a little better.

Johnny was next in line. I felt real scared for him. He climbed up on that big scary guy's lap. Johnny didn't even look scared. He whispered something in Santa's ear. Santa winked at Johnny. Santa looked at me and smiled. I felt lots better. No more barf.

Johnny jumped off Santa's lap.

"What did you ask for?" I asked.

Johnny smiled. "It's a secret," he said.

Except that was weird. 'Cause Johnny doesn't ever smile at me. He must've asked Santa for something real good. Except maybe he told Santa to bring me a lump of coal. He probably wanted pay back. 'Cause I drowned Larry. I bet that's why Johnny was so smiley.

9. Christmas Morning

I made sure I was the bestest kid ever for the next three days.

On Christmas Eve, Mom and Dad let me and Johnny open one gift each. We both got pajamas from Grandma. I thought that was a real stupid gift. Mine had reindeers all over the place. Johnny's had soccer balls on them. I would have rather had a neat toy. Except Mom told me to be thankful for my new pajamas. So I tried. Except my brain still wished for a neat toy.

"Go put your pajamas on, boys," Mom and Dad said. "And get to bed. Or Santa won't come."

I ran to my room real fast. I put those new stiff reindeer pajamas on. Then I jumped in bed. I covered my head way far up with the blankets.

Mom came in to kiss me goodnight.

"Do you think Santa will come, Mom?" I asked.

"I don't know," said Mom. "Have you been a good boy?"

"Not really," I said.

Mom giggled. "I think Santa will understand. He's a pretty nice guy."

I hoped Mom knew what she was talking about.

I stayed awake under my blankets. 'Cause I wanted to hear Santa's sleigh bells. It was real dark in my bedroom. I didn't hear anything. I fell asleep for a little bit. Except then I woke up. I listened. Except there were no sleigh bells. I fell asleep again. Then a tapping noise woke me up. I wondered if it was those reindeers up on top of the roof.

Knock, Knock, Knock... Somebody was knocking on my bedroom door. OH NO! What if it was Santa?

"Jake the Snake, are you awake?"

"Is that you, Santa?" I asked kind of nervous.

What if that big scary guy was going to deliver that lump of coal right to my bedroom? What if I barfed on him again?

"No, Stupid Kid! It's me."

WHEW! It was just Johnny.

"I'm awake," I answered.

Johnny opened my bedroom door. Then he turned the light on. I squinted my eyes at him.

"Get out of bed, already! It's Christmas morning! Let's see if Santa came!" Johnny yelled.

I jumped out of bed real fast. I ran down the steps real quick with Johnny. Except when I ran, my stomach felt real flippy floppy. 'Cause my brain wondered how big that lump of coal was going to be. Except maybe Mom was right. Maybe Santa forgave me.

We ran into the living room. There was a little box next to the tree. It had my name on it. And Johnny's too.

My brain thought it was that stupid lump of coal.

"Open it," Johnny told me.

I think he was scared.

So I opened it. Real slow. And guess what? It wasn't even a stupid lump of coal. It was a stupid piece of paper instead.

Johnny ripped it out of my hand, "It's a letter from Santa!"

"A letter from Santa?" I asked.

"Yeah!" Johnny said. "Look!"

The letter was typed real neat. Except I didn't even know Santa could type. I bet Mrs. Claus typed it. Or maybe one of the elves. Or maybe a North Pole Mom.

"Read it, Johnny!" I said. "'Cause I can't even read!"

Johnny read:

"Dear Johnny and Jake the Snake:

I couldn't squeeze your presents down the chimney, so I put them in the garage.

Sincerely, S. Claus"

I wondered how big that lump of coal was going to be. 'Cause even Santa can squeeze down the chimney. And he's a real fat guy.

We ran real fast to the garage. We opened the garage door. There was a big square thing. It was covered with a big plastic bag. It looked like one of those bags Dad puts in the trash can. After he takes the old smelly trash out. That big square thing had a red bow on top. Plus it had my name on it. My brain wondered if Santa had big square lumps of coal up at the North Pole. I was real scared. So I pulled that plastic stuff off real slow. My stomach was real bad flippy floppy. I felt like I was going to barf all over the place. Just like I did in that tall mall elf's jingle bell hat. Except I didn't.

Then I pulled the rest of the plastic stuff off. I couldn't even believe my own eyes. Cause guess why? It was a big square sand table with a bunch of sand inside! Plus right in the middle of all that sand was a plastic cage. Inside that cage was a real cool lizard with a curly tail. It was even cooler than dead Larry!

"Look, Johnny! Santa brought you a lizard! Look at its curly tail!"

"Awesome! It's a chameleon!" Johnny yelled. Then the surprising part happened. Johnny hugged me.

"Wow! What a cool sand table!" Johnny said. "I think Santa forgave you, Jake the Snake!"

"That's 'cause I asked him to bring you a new lizard," I told Johnny, "'Cause I'm real sorry Larry is deader than a doornail."

Johnny looked at me real surprised. “You asked Santa to bring me a new lizard?” he asked.

“Yep,” I said, “when I barfed in that mall elf’s hat.”

“I asked Santa to bring you a sand table too,” Johnny said. “I told him you didn’t mean to be bad all the time. You just can’t help it. ’Cause you’re a little kid.”

I gave Johnny a real big hug. “You’re the bestest big brother ever!”

Johnny rolled his eyes. “You don’t have to be all mushy, Jake the Snake!” he said.

Mom and Dad walked in the garage. “What’s all the commotion?” they asked.

“Santa came!” I yelled.

“Wow!” said Mom. “I can’t believe it!”

Dad winked. “Why don’t we go inside and open our other gifts?” he said.

I thought that was the bestest idea ever.

“I think Santa left some gifts behind the tree,” Mom said.

I gave Mom a real big hug.

“What was that for?” Mom asked.

“’Cause I’m real happy Santa didn’t bring me a new North Pole Mom.”

Mom smiled, “I love you, Jake the Snake!”

“I love you too, Mom!” I said.

We got a bunch of real cool gifts. Plus Santa even brought me a fancy suit jacket and church tie. Now Mom couldn’t even be mad anymore! I thought Santa was a real smart guy.

Santa even brought Mom some new smelly lotion. Plus he brought Dad a whole pack of handkerchiefs. They didn't even have snot on them yet. I thought those would make real good flags for my sandcastles.

Santa brought Johnny some new markers that weren't dried up. Plus he got some new video games for time-out in his bedroom. Everyone was real happy. Especially me. 'Cause I didn't even get no stupid lump of coal. Plus no new North Pole Mom. And I didn't even have to sit in that stupid time-out chair one time on Christmas! Plus Johnny let me play with Carl the Chameleon. And I let Johnny put Carl in my new sand. Except Carl pooped in there. So we had to scoop it out. But I didn't mind. 'Cause it was the bestest day of my whole entire life. It's just too bad every day ain't Christmas.